SCOUT and ACE

The Scary Bear

Written by Rose Impey
Illustrated by Ant Parker

KU-710-133

ORCHARD BOOKS

Once upon a time, our heroes,

SCOUT and **ACE**

set out on a trip

into outer, outer-space.

Sucked through a worm-hole . . .

to a strange, new place,

lost in a galaxy called Fairy Tale Space.

"What's that bear doing there?" says Scout.

Ace doesn't know, but he says,
"Let's find out."

They fly closer to the bear.

A bit too close!

The bear lives in the barrel,
floating in space.
But he's bored with his barrel.

Scout and Ace feel sorry
for the bear.

They invite him onto
their spaceship.
Just for a visit.

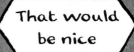
That would
be nice

The bear has never been on a spaceship before.

But he's soon bored with that, too.

"Grrr!" The bear grumbles and groans.
"It's not fair! *I* want a chair," he moans.

Ace lets the bear have *his* chair.
The bear likes to get his
own way.

Scout tells Ace, "Don't worry.
It's only for today."

But the bear is bored again.
Next he wants Scout's chair.

. . . he gets his own way.

Ace tells Scout, "Don't worry.
It's only for today."

Once the bear has got Scout's chair, he wants to do Scout's job too.

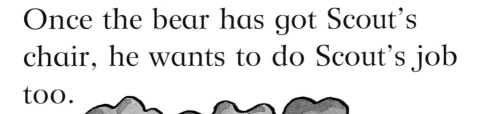

I want to steer

But *he's* never steered a spaceship . . .

. . . and he doesn't have clue.

Scout and Ace feel as if the bear
has hijacked the SuperStar.

"We have to get rid of that bear,"
Ace tells Scout.
But how are they going to get
him out?

Soon the bear is bored again.

He tells Scout and Ace he is bored with being Captain. He wants to be King of Space.

At last Scout and Ace have
a plan.

"We have got a throne," says Ace,
with a grin on his face.
"Would your highness like to try
it out?" asks Scout.

They sit him in the ejector seat.
And they give the bear a crown.

When the bear is sitting
comfortably, Ace pulls the
handle down.

Scout and Ace are free of the bear. Now they can get the SuperStar back on track.

Great shot!

"What did the scary bear take on his trip?" asks Ace. "All the bare essentials! Boom! Boom!"

Scout groans. "Must be time to get out of here," he moans.

Fire the engines...

and lower the dome.

Once more our heroes...

are heading for home.

ABERDEEN
CITY
LIBRARIES

Enjoy all these stories about

SCOUT and ACE
and their adventures in Space!

Scout and Ace: Kippers for Supper
1 84362 163 0

Scout and Ace: Flying in a Frying Pan
1 84362 164 9

Scout and Ace: Stuck on Planet Gloo
1 84362 165 7

Scout and Ace: Kissing Frogs
1 84362 168 1

Scout and Ace: Talking Tables
1 84362 166 5

Scout and Ace: A Cat, a Rat and a Bat
1 84362 167 3

Scout and Ace: Three Heads to Feed
1 84362 169 X

Scout and Ace: The Scary Bear
1 84362 170 3

All priced at £8.99 each.

Colour Crunchies are available from all good bookshops, or can be ordered direct from the publisher:
Orchard Books, PO BOX 29, Douglas MM99 1BQ.
Credit card orders please telephone 01624 836000 or fax 01624 837033
or email: bookshop@enterprise.net for details.

To order please quote title, author and ISBN and your full name and address. Cheques and postal
orders should be made payable to 'Bookpost plc'. Postage and packing is FREE within the UK -
overseas customers should add £1.00 per book. Prices and availability are subject to change.

ORCHARD BOOKS, 96 Leonard Street, London EC2A 4XD.
Hachette Children's Books, Level 17-207 Kent Street, Sydney, NSW 2000.
This edition first published in Great Britain in hardback in 2005. First paperback publication 2006.
Text © Rose Impey 2005. Illustrations © Ant Parker 2005. The rights of Rose Impey to be identified as
the author and Ant Parker to be identified as the illustrator have been asserted by them in accordance with the
Copyright, Designs and Patents Act, 1988. A CIP catalogue record for this book is available from the British Library.
ISBN 1 84362 170 3   10 9 8 7 6 5 4 3 2 1
Printed in China